URBANIA

By L.A. Story

DEDICATION

This novella is dedicated to those out there who fight the good fight every day to maintain the right for all of us to be individuals.

TABLE OF CONTENTS

DEDICATION

TABLE OF CONTENTS

URBANIA

ABOUT THE AUTHOR

ACKNOWLEDGEMENTS

COMING SOON

COPYRIGHT NOTICE

URBANIA

My taxi stopped at the curb in front of Urbania's massive gates. I grabbed my bag off the seat next to me, got out, closed the door and then stood for a long moment with my hand on the car's roof -- keeping in touch with what was left of my world.

The desert's summer sun painted me in late afternoon glow. I gaped at the gate and an arid breeze snaked its way into my mouth, French-kissed me and ruffled my hair.

Urbania -- a mysterious city enclosed by a fifty foot brick wall like the ancient Jericho of Biblical fame. Urbania's only entrance was a mammoth gate that looked very much like a metal tapestry of loosely woven iron lace embellished with glittering, sculpted rods of gold and silver.

I recalled the legend that the gate was not to seal in Urbania's seven-million inhabitants -- but to keep the rest of the world out. Urbania liked her secrets.

I spoke to the taxi driver through the open passenger window, "Please, wait for me a moment."

The driver ignored my request. He gave the Great City's entrance a fearful glance just before he screeched away from the curb and left me stranded.

I clenched my fist in an effort not to shout after him. The city's guards missed nothing and they would have to be convinced of my sincerity if I were to be allowed to enter. This sincerity would certainly be doubted if the guards saw me run after my taxi -- begging the driver to stop.

I scanned the area in front of the gate and saw fifteen Sentinels, ten men and five women -- all dressed in the same type of uniform, which consisted of a black, belted robe with a gold tunic and black pants beneath. Each guard had a different insignia embroidered in gold on his/her shoulders and back. The pants were tucked into black combat boots. The guards managed to look both elegant and deadly.

The guards were painted golden-pink by the sunset glow. The romanticism of the color did not dispel their menace. I chose to address the guard nearest where I stood on the cobbled sidewalk. I got within nine feet of him when he raised his rifle and pointed it at my chest. I dropped my bag at my feet and raised my hands above my head.

"What is your business here, foreigner?"

I tried to remember what I was supposed to do. "I want to enter the gates of Urbania," I said as clear and fierce as I could under the circumstances.

Fear coiled inside me like an asp. I needed this to work in my favor for more than one reason and I scanned my memory for the last news report of a petitioner being shot at Urbania's gates. It seemed it had been at least three years. I did not know whether to be relieved or worried -- Urbania might be due for another intruder assassination.

The guard looked me up and down. I wondered what he saw.

I tried to picture myself from his point of view -- a thirty-something man who looked athletic (if a bit soft); above-average height. I considered my other features through the guard's eyes -- big shoulders, slight paunch, pleasant face, dark blonde hair and hazel eyes.

After my personal assessment of what I thought the guard would see, I decided he would not be all that impressed. Hell, neither was I. In any case, I could not tell what the guard thought as his expression was carefully blank.

"What gifts would you offer our city?" The guard asked.

"I am a writer," I stated, simply. I knew this would win points, although I left out that I was not the literary type -- I was a journalist. That snippet of information would get me shot on site.

Urbania did not take kindly to those who would rob her of her precious secrets. Much blood had been shed before the city gates -- on the cobbled sidewalk -- in the seventy-five years since the city was established.

"A wriiiiiteeeeeer," the guard repeated. His face still held no expression, but he said "writer" soft and slow as if it tasted like the richest chocolate. After a moment, he said, "Why would you leave the world and become a Great Citizen?"

I knew this was critical. Ketch had told me so. My fear, combined with a dusty memory from a college drama class, served nicely to cause me to tremble. I managed to work up some tears (my growing terror made this easier). Ketch had told me to use as much truth as I could in what I said. This would help make the sincerity ring clearer.

"I'm tired of the world ....or maybe it's grown tired of me. I've dreamed of this place -- dreamed of it ever since I was a small boy. I'm sick to death of forced traditions, religion, conditional love, hatred and the leash that is our government -- it has choked me. I just want the peace and freedom to be who I am ... please ... please ... don't deny me this chance," I sobbed.

My heart raced. My tears were suddenly true and that frightened me.

I lowered my hands and fell to my knees, prostrate, before the guard and his fourteen comrades. I cried into the cobblestones, "Please let me in ... I have no other home."

With my face so close to the sidewalk, I could see there were bloodstains in the mortar between the stones. I shivered.

My God, what made me think I wanted this so badly? Was a story worth risking my life? But, I knew it was worth it. Urbania was the story of the century. I felt the press of a gun barrel to my temple. The guard now stood over me.

The guard asked softly, "What did you see ... when you dreamed of Urbania?" His voice came from high above me. I did not dare look up.

My tale of the dreams had been true a long time ago; I desperately raked the coals of my mind to stir the memory. After a moment, there was a quick impatient prod from the gun barrel at my temple.

"I dreamed of a creature with gleaming eyes that creeps around at night. I never see it full-on but I remember its eyes as it chases me through a field, where I'm running blind. ... I also remember a woman with black hair ... she protects me ..." my voice trailed off. I simply could not remember much more than that.

The guard above me was quiet. I got the impression he was looking or signaling the other Sentinels. He taunted, "Your dream has impressed me, foreigner, but we can't just let you pass the gate so easily. You might get the impression that Urbania's guards are easy like whores."

The others chuckled. I spared a brief glance up and found it strange -- laughter without smiling.

"I think you need to earn your way in ... maybe by performing some menial task ..." Above me, the guard's tone was thoughtful.

My terror expanded. I felt I had lost the battle.

"I know ..." the guard said. He came to stand directly in front of me. "I think my boots need to be cleaned. I want you to clean them, foreigner."

"Whatever you want," I said with a glance up at the towering figure.

The guard managed a small smile -- the first expression I had seen cross his features -- and my own fear nauseated me.

There was something else. For a moment, I thought I saw a strange pinpoint of golden light where the guard's iris should be. It was gone before I could be sure.

I raised a hand to brush the guard's boots -- an award-winning journalist on my knees preparing to clean a man's boots with my bare hands. To keep my mind off what I was about to do, I mentally drafted my acceptance speech for the Pulitzer. The guard abruptly moved his foot from my reach.

"No, foreigner," he said as he leaned down to address me. "I want you to lick them. Lick my boots clean like the dog you are."

I felt my face blanch. My jaw tightened and the guard saw it, unfortunately. The gun's barrel slid from my temple and down the side of my face. The barrel was jammed painfully against my jaw.

The guard spoke low. "I guess you don't want to enter Urbania's gates badly enough."

"Then you don't know me too damn well, do you?" I rose up on my knees and screamed at him, surprising myself as well as him. "You can't keep me from it! I want to be part of Urbania!"

The guard put his boot back within my reach. "Prove it."

I clenched my jaw in a lingering moment of stubbornness. My chest heaved. I breathed heavily through my nose and fought back the throat-swelling thickness of tears. My eyes did not tear up, but my nose ran. I un-tucked my shirt and used it to wipe my face.

I lowered myself back down to my hands and knees. I stared at the boot closest to me and finally I brought my face close. When I decided to do it, I went all the way. It was the way I did everything. "In for a penny, in for a pound."…As my foster mother would have said. So, there were no delicate, timid strokes of the tongue. I licked the guard's boot clean of its light dusting of desert dirt with long, lapping strokes.

Like a dog.

There was no drafting of any speeches to escape the moment. I blanked everything out of my mind -- I simply drifted off to some neutral place as I often did as a child. I did not allow myself to taste the dirt and I tried to block out the reality of grit as it was slowly insinuated between my teeth and backed up in my throat.

When I was done with both boots, I instinctively knew spitting on the cobbled sidewalk would not be taken lightly, so I swallowed with the same blankness of mind I employed during the cleaning process.

When I finished, I sat back on my haunches and glared up at the guard. He nodded slowly at the next guard in line. The woman approached. Her face was not so neutral. What slight emotion I read indicated she did not approve, but she also looked resolved to follow orders.

With a series of hand motions, the male guard signaled the others to spread out. He motioned for the woman to come closer.

"Now, clean her boots as you did mine, foreigner," he ordered.

I crawled on all fours to the woman. I lowered myself to her right boot and repeated what I had done before. I briefly wondered if she could feel the strokes of my tongue through the thick material of her boot ... then I closed my mind off.

My tongue was dirty and dry by the time I began to lick her second boot. The dirt choked me. I desperately needed a drink of water. I did not even have enough spit to swallow. Most of what I managed to do on the second boot was smear the dirt around with my filthy tongue. I did the best I could and then sat back on my haunches.

"Have any more cleaning for me to do, Sir?" I said. My voice was an odd, dirt-choked croak.

The guard considered me for a long moment, and then slowly shook his head. "No, that won't be necessary."

He signaled the woman and another guard, "Indigo and Saul, assist the foreigner up."

The two Sentinels each grabbed one of my arms and hauled me to my feet. I wondered if the "head" guard was about to execute me. I managed to numb my mind enough to accept anything.

"What are you called, foreigner?"

"Richard Shelton," I rasped.

"I am Nestor, Richard Shelton. Welcome to Urbania," he said with a gracious bow. Then he turned and sent out the call, "Open the gate, we have a new citizen!"

Urbania's mammoth gate shuddered on its tracks as it began to slide. I watched in wonder as the gate opened and I thought it was the most beautiful sight I had ever seen.

A peculiar shiver brushed its wings over my flesh as we walked past the opened gate.

There was another brick wall directly behind the gate, which blocked any view a petitioner might hope to glimpse of The Great City. This wall extended just past the gate's width on each side.

Nestor, Indigo and Saul escorted me the length of the wall then we stepped around it and I laid eyes upon Urbania for the first time.

My knees nearly buckled. I was suddenly grateful for the two Sentinels that held my arms. What was before me was not what I had expected. I had done my research well and I knew the city was populated at least five or six generations ago by the best of the best -- artists, writers, sculptors, philosophers and scientists -- and all were idealists. The city was populated now by the brilliant offspring of those original colonists.

I had expected an artist colony full of hand-made adobe homes or perhaps some ancient long-houses. Ketch had never described the city to me. I had asked him on many occasions and I could tell he wanted to tell me but the words would never form. His mouth worked silently but words never came and he'd only end up staring out the window of his tiny apartment -- the one that overlooked the dingy, colorless city in which he now lived.

He would be helpless for at least an hour afterward. The effort of trying to describe The Great City was too much for him. Now I knew why. Urbania could not be accurately described although I knew someday I would try.

Urbania was a pure and glaring white -- an alabaster city -- ancient and modern at the same time. The streets were meticulously inlaid with mosaic tiles created in designs that were not only intricate and beautiful, but also mathematically astounding in their geometry and color -- a sparkling, white city interwoven with rich, multi-colored streets like festooning ribbons.

I felt a finger pushing up under my chin to close my mouth. Startled, I sheepishly looked at the guard called Indigo, whose boots I had licked. I had been engaged in blatant gawking.

As our odd quartet proceeded further into the city, I watched the heavy foot traffic along the luxurious streets and I endured the stares of dozens of people -- all races -- and they seemed to move in an uncanny harmony. Their combined voices had a lilting, almost lullaby-like quality unlike a typical urban hum. Their garments were made of light weight fabrics. The colors were brilliant and the variety was vast. It seemed too quiet to me for such a large population until I realized what I was missing -- automobiles. There was not one in sight.

The buildings around me were all sharply cornered and strangely seamless as if the entire building had been simply carved out of an alabaster-looking stone or marble and none seemed to top more than a dozen floors in height, but I knew I had not yet seen much of the city. It reminded me of a clean, wistful fantasy version of New Orleans.

There were elaborate balconies with intricate wrought-iron railings and opulent parapets inlaid with colored stones. One of the biggest shocks I received was the amount of vegetation. Urbania was a city that now took up a good portion of the Nevada desert. Plants as lush and green as I now observed should not exist to this extent. Plants grew in pots and hung in baskets everywhere there was space. It reminded me of all the stories I ever heard about the hanging gardens of Babylon.

I was enthralled and moved almost to tears by the beauty all around me. This city was not tourist trap. They invited no one, needed no one and rarely wanted anyone new inside their heavily guarded gate and I was getting the rarest of glimpses.

We followed Nestor to the nearest building. An elaborately etched glass door slid open at our approach. Once inside, I was amazed again. The inner walls were a deep, Goldenrod yellow. Pure … it looked as if the color was part of the material with which the building had been constructed. The interior of the room we entered appeared to be a waiting room of sorts as I noted the long, colorful couches and low tables.

Nestor left me with my deadly babysitters for a moment as he disappeared into another room off to the left. When Nestor returned, he was accompanied by a petite woman. She was youngish, or perhaps her slight statue provided that illusion and the most striking thing about her by far, was that she was completely bald. Her scalp was bare of hair and studded instead with small golden loops, each of which sported a tiny, dangling teardrop diamond. Her scalp sparkled with the tiny, glittering ornaments. She wore a lime green garment that looked very much like an Indian sari. The material was extremely unusual. I couldn't decide what it was -- something like silk, only more lustrous. There were several layers to make the garment opaque.

"Richard Shelton, this is Shara. She will be your translator. She will teach you about The Great City and all of our laws and traditions. You would do well to listen to her," Nestor advised.

Shara looked at me with luminous, sapphire eyes. "You need water."

My mouth was too dry to speak and she had made a statement; not asked a question, I noted. I nodded my response.

Without preamble, the sentinels left me alone with Shara. She motioned for me to follow her through the doorway from which she had entered. We moved down a long hallway … the smooth, seamless lines of the architecture made me feel claustrophobic, as if I were in a tomb. Shara moved in a complete and unnerving silence -- there was not even a rustle from her garment.

The only sound she made was when we walked about halfway down the hall and she turned her head to the right as we turned to enter another short hall. In that moment, with the extreme movement of her head, the diamonds tapped softly together. A pair of frosted glass doors slid open as we approached. I began to wonder if there were any traditional doors in Urbania.

Beyond the doors was an enormous, vaulted room -- the Goldenrod yellow walls from the waiting room and the hall faded to aqua. The room was steamy and filled with plants and pleasant herbal aromas. In the center was a huge, steaming pool. There were people bathing … and being bathed … thoroughly. I averted my eyes as I followed Shara through the bathhouse.

We went through another set of frosted glass doors and down yet another hallway. We were swiftly lost somewhere within the bowels of the building. I never felt so helpless. The twists and turns disoriented me. I had to trust this stranger or I would get lost. It was hard -- not knowing what would happen next.

I conjured up my Pulitzer fantasy to calm my jitters.

How far are you willing to go, Richard? How badly do you want to see Urbania? No one else has lived to give out any details. Ketch's voice haunted me now in my worst hour. It was something he had asked me one sunny afternoon. He was most talkative on clear, sunny days. He seemed to feel safer then. He would stare out one of those dirty windows near his favorite chair and he'd unconsciously twist his hands together -- strong-looking hands but curiously dirty beneath the nails, greasy dirt, like a mechanic. He was a recluse. I always wondered about those nails.

Now, I knew I was in danger but I had something the other reporters did not -- the advice of an insider. Ketch was the only of Urbania's few escapees that managed to survive, for all the good it did him. It was funny how I could picture him clearly -- as if I were still sitting in his tiny living room and shoving aside one of his five cats to make room for myself on the sofa as Ketch sat in his favorite lounge chair and stared out the damn windows.

Ketch watched for something. He was convinced that The Receivers would find him. The Receivers -- he called them "dream-rapists" and "mind crushers." He only referred to them a couple of times with a fearful glance about him as he spoke.

He warned me about several things to watch for in Urbania: The Transmitters, The Receivers … and nightfall. Nights terrified Ketch. Despite his fear, Ketch wanted something and he agreed to help me if I helped him get back the only thing he wanted from Urbania -- Ivey. I had to find Ketch's Ivey.

Presently, Shara indicated a door (a traditional-looking door) to our right. This door did not slide open automatically. Shara had to press her hand to a control panel. We stepped past the threshold and I found myself in an unpleasant orange room. I knew immediately that this was a medical room of sorts.

Its furniture items strongly resembled traditional medical equipment. I saw an examination chair. A nervous jitter took up residence in my belly. I felt nauseated. I didn't care for the potential of this development.

Shara instructed me to join her at a wash basin situated in one corner. She held her hand beneath a porcelain spout and water poured gently over her waiting fingers. She smiled at me. "Now you do it, Richard Shelton. Rinse your mouth and drink."

I did so, gratefully, as I cleansed my mouth and quenched my thirst. Afterward, I turned back to Shara. I wondered what was next.

"You must disrobe for inspection," she said, solemnly.

"Inspection?"

She nodded and the diamonds tapped together, prettily. The sound eased some of the fear her words caused. The door to the corridor opened and three men and one woman entered. Shara acknowledged the group with a slight nod. When her glance swung back to me, it was not without sympathy. "You must disrobe for inspection, Richard Shelton. This is not optional."

I felt my face flush but, once again, I shut off my mind as I began to unbutton my untucked shirt and slipped off my shoes. Briefly, I wondered at the time. I knew nightfall was closing in ... I had to find Ivey. This was one point that Ketch had been adamant about or the whole plan was blown before it began.

"Ivey will help you hide from The Receivers -- they only come out at night. If you do not know how to hide from them, you won't survive to write your story," Ketch had said.

Presently, as I undressed, I desperately wished I had worked out more and eaten a few less hot dogs, but was more worried about what they intended to do. I stripped down to my underwear and socks and I waited.

"You must disrobe completely," said one of the men -- a tall, stern-looking fellow with a big nose.

I felt my face grow hot as I pulled off my socks. I looked like an uncoordinated Yoga enthusiast. Finally, I shoved down my underwear and stepped out. I stood straight and tried not to look as frightened and vulnerable as I felt. I cupped my hands in front of my privates.

How far are you willing to go? Ketch's voice haunted.

"Come," the big-nosed man said, tersely. He indicated a chair that looked much like one I would see in a dentist's office.

I noticed no one in the group wore the standard disposable gloves I was used to seeing on medical personnel.

After I settled into the seat, I let out a cry of alarm as my arms and legs were suddenly strapped down. The lower portion divided and my legs were spread as the chair reclined. The chair was raised to suit the group's standing position.

"They will get this over with as quickly as possible," Shara reassured me. She stepped back and quietly watched.

A dark-haired man approached and used an unpleasant-looking object to prop open my jaw while he proceeded to probe around and in between my teeth with a sharp instrument. He hit a couple of sensitive spots and I cried out in pain. My fingers gripped the arm rests of the chair. While he worked at my teeth, I felt the hands of the others -- ungloved hands -- cold, warm, clammy, and dry all over my body. They kneaded and examined every inch as they ran fingers through my hair, rubbed my scalp and poked into my ears.

A small, flexible tube the size of a straw was run up my nose and down my throat. My eyes watered at the discomfort and I gagged reflexively. I felt a hand take my penis into a firm grip and as a slender catheter was inserted. I could not stop the whimper that escaped me and it was followed by a near scream at the burning pain. They were not being gentle.

I tried to look at what was being done but my head was immobilized. My legs were spread further and I felt an object being inserted into the only orifice left that they had not yet violated. I yelped and tensed up.

The oral probing abruptly ceased and the tube in my nose was withdrawn. The catheter in my penis gave me a fierce and painful urge to urinate. The other probe in my southern-most region was going deeper and became more uncomfortable by the second. I moaned and tears sprang to my eyes. In that moment, I hated them -- hated them all!

I managed to raise my head a bit and I could see the woman standing between my spread thighs and I realized that she and the other doctors were not just probing -- they were studying a screen above the chair. They had inserted tiny cameras inside me and were having a look around.

I almost cried with my relief when the objects were withdrawn after a few moments.

Finally, I could not contain the question any longer, "Why?"

The others ignored me -- which only added to the humiliating and dehumanizing experience. They went about their business putting away equipment and washing up. Shara stepped forward to raise me to a sitting position and lower the chair. She unstrapped my arms and legs as she answered my question. "They were looking for recording devices and other contraband."

"They thought they'd find a recorder up my *ass*?" I asked bitterly as I got up off of the chair.

Shara's lips twitched. "You'd be surprised what we've found and where we found it."

I fell silent. What could I say? Was I not also going to extreme measures to get inside Urbania?

"Of course, those traitors were either, executed, imprisoned or exiled," Shara said as she turned away. With a strange flap of her fingers, she indicated that I should follow her.

I hesitated as I realized she expected me to follow her as I was -- naked.

"Where are my clothes?"

She stopped and looked back at me. "You are a citizen of Urbania -- The Great City. You will be clothed as such. We take care of our people. First, you must be bathed. It is our way to bathe a foreigner to rid him of the stench of The World."

Naked, like a scene from a nightmare, I followed Shara back to the bathhouse and the enormous pool. There were wide, semi-circle steps leading down into the steaming, blue-green water and Shara directed me to step down into the bathing pool. There was a heavy herbal aroma wafting up from the water -- intense and heady.

My skin tingled as I slowly wandered in until immersed to my waist in warm water. Shara stood at the pool's edge and called forth one of the many, silent bustling attendants. A woman separated from the group and approached us with her face downcast. Her long, dark hair was pulled back into a loose braid but enough errant tresses had come loose to fall forward and conceal her down-turned features. She wore a soft-looking robe and held a tray laden with, what appeared to be, bathing accoutrements.

After a nod from Shara, the woman knelt to place the tray in the water, where it floated and bobbed with the gentle waves. She stood and removed her robe, revealing a beautiful body … gently curved, creamy skin and long legs …

She descended the steps and grasped one of the tray's handles and drew it with her as she approached me. I watched her -- mesmerized.

"Do not speak to her," Shara cautioned. I thought I detected a note of snobbery in her tone. "She is a Breaker – an indentured servant of The City. Her name is Ivey and she can only communicate with authorized personnel."

Ivey. I could not believe it! Ketch had said she would find me before dark, but how he knew this was a mystery to me.

Presently, Ivey raised her face and looked directly at me with the most compelling brown eyes I had ever seen. I noted several things simultaneously. She was beautiful, she was intelligent, she was defiant … and she was disfigured.

My eyes drifted along her face to take in details like her beautifully sculpted features, her dark eyes, her dark hair carried a few shining strands of silver and the ugly, puckered scar shaped like a "B" in the center of her forehead. The scar's shape made it undeniable that this disfigurement had been done to her deliberately. I assumed the "B" stood for "Breaker," whatever that meant. I glanced around at the other servants. None were scarred as Ivey was. Ivey's gaze was direct and intense, despite her humble status.

After a moment, she looked away and began to gather cloths and scented gels. She took me by the shoulders and gently urged me to turn around and place my hands on the pools' edge. I did so and she began to work the soap into the skin of my back and shoulders. Her hands moved with a soothing and practiced skill.

Her gentle touch calmed me and after a few moments I was almost drowsy as her hands cleansed every part of my backside. Carefully, she turned me around and worked another gel into my face. She urged me to dip my face into the fragrant water for rinsing. I did so and she indicated I completely immerse my head to wet my hair. I obeyed and she worked a mint-scented cleanser into my scalp and hair. I was surprised when there was no lather.

Again, she silently requested that I dip my head beneath the water to rinse. I leaned forward to do so and this brought me distractingly close to her breasts. I thought about her breasts as my head went beneath the water. She held my head there with a light touch. I began to panic until I felt her fingers explore my face. She nimbly slipped an object into my mouth. I tucked the tiny package under my tongue and met her eyes when I surfaced. Her mysterious dark eyes revealed nothing but the reflection of my own questioning expression.

The bath was over and as we were moving from the water, Ivey took a chance and whispered, "Swallow that before lights out. You won't survive The Receivers if you don't."

Moments later, Ivey helped me dress after a thorough drying -- I gritted my teeth to fight the natural reaction of arousal. Then, with a bow, she picked up her robe and bath tray and disappeared back into the quietly bustling mob of servants.

A soft tap on my shoulder reminded me that I was supposed to follow Shara. I turned to look at her.

"Come, Richard Shelton," she said with a bright smile. "It's time to take you to your new home."

It was dark as we stepped out onto the street. There were no streetlights and the night was very dark. Shara's garment was a light-colored specter for me to follow. I heard a distant jingle -- a cheery alarm behind us, toward the city's gates. I stopped and turned. Shara sensed the moment I stopped. I felt her hand on my arm -- a tentative touch in the darkness...

"Wait, Richard Shelton. That's the night bell. There will be lights soon."

My heart began to pound faster as a memory came to me. I knew what this was! I had forgotten my history!

Before Urbania walled itself off from the rest of "The World," it allowed satellites to observe its activities, which included an evening procedure that became famous. The moment full dark fell, Urbania would chase away the night. Beginning at the city's entrance, the lights would wink on and roll like a wave across the city until all of Urbania was lit up like a star in the Nevada desert. I recalled seeing video footage of the nightly event. No one had seen this fantastic tradition in over 20 years, not since Urbania had attacked and destroyed any satellites that were trained on it.

Now, I stood and watched, with unhinged jaw, as an astounding flood of light began at the gates and moved in a wave toward me as buildings, side streets, walkways and walls lit up with a glow that appeared to originate from within. The wave came at me and rushed past. I was suddenly awash in light of all colors and the wave rolled on until all of Urbania was lit up like glory.

I laughed my amazement. Citizens strolling nearby flashed bewildered smiles at my wonder. I turned to see Shara staring at me. A tiny smile played about her lips. She looked around her, perhaps taking in all the beauty as if through my eyes. She sighed and shook her head -- diamonds tapped prettily. "Urbania has a flair for the dramatic."

A moment later she abruptly turned away from me. "Let us get you to your new home, Richard Shelton."

I followed her through a twist of glowing, multi-colored streets until we reached a three-story structure.

Another automatic sliding door opened to admit us to the ground floor. I followed her up the stairs and eventually she led me to a large apartment with a balcony that overlooked the street. The apartment was already furnished with everything I would need. Everything about the apartment was familiar as what I would see in "The World," but Urbania had its own version.

The first room we stepped into was a spacious living room area with comfortable-looking couches. There was a kitchen area with a strange-looking stove I had no idea how to use and there was a simple, glass front ice box -- already stocked with food.

The only bedroom in the apartment was enormous and included a dresser and a large bed. There was a bathroom in the hall.

"Everything you need is here except for clothes. We will get more for you in the marketplace tomorrow."

"What about my bag?"

"There was a recording device found there … you cannot have it back."

"*Recording device*? No there was not …" I hesitated. "You mean my notebook and pen?"

"Recording devices." Shara repeated, firmly.

"But, I'm a writer. How can I contribute to The Great City without pen and paper?"

"You will contribute and create and it will become part of the Mindstream. That is how you will give to The Great City. It's far more efficient … thoughts and images are so pure. How many times have you set out to write something only to have it fall short of what you envisioned? That does not happen here. The Receivers collect the visions, untainted. You'll learn … give it time."

Shara bade me goodnight after she informed me she'd be back to fetch me in the morning.

After Shara left, I wandered the apartment, trailing my fingers along the white alabaster-like walls as I walked from room to room. I realized I was hungry and returned to the kitchen to poke around. I found containers in the cabinets and food in the ice box. I composed a supper of cheese, crackers and fruit. I got water from the spigot and hoped Urbania's filtration system was as superior as Urbanians were supposed to be.

I took my meal out to the balcony and settled into one of a pair of wood chairs. I watched the passing foot traffic below as I ate. I did not realize how exhausted I was until I jerked awake in my chair later.

I was not certain how long I had slept (I did not think it could have been very long) but there was no more pedestrian traffic below. I figured it had to be close to "lights out." Suddenly, I remembered the tiny package Ivey had given me at the bathhouse. I had slipped it from my mouth and palmed it into one of the pockets in my loose trousers on the way to the apartment. The package was wrapped in a tiny bit of waxy paper and when I opened it I found a little green pill. I hoped I had not waited too long. I popped the pill in my mouth and swallowed it with the scant remains of my water -- an act of faith.

I wondered when "lights out" occurred and what the procedure was. Just as the thought passed through my mind, the lights went out and I was plunged into a complete blackness.

A primitive fear stole over me and I forced myself to wait a few moments until my eyes adjusted to the vague glow of moonlight that now dimly illuminated the streets that had glowed so beautifully only moments before. Finally, I felt comfortable enough to stand and I shuffled tentatively to the balcony's rail, where I looked down at the street.

The city was almost completely silent but here and there a shuffle of footsteps could be heard below, or an impassioned moan or the softest of whispers -- someone had not completed their thoughts for the day and wanted to voice them before drifting off to sleep.

Ivey's pill began to affect me. It was just a vague, heaviness of limb but I knew it would get stronger. I would have to make my way to the bed before it fully took me over.

I was about to turn away from the balcony rail when I caught a glimpse of … something … something moving swiftly into the alley several buildings down from mine. It was not much of a glimpse, just a deeper shadow among shadows.

A lone female walked the sidewalk below. Her pace was brisk, like a teenager out after curfew and trying desperately not to get caught. I must have made a sound or a subtle movement but I caught her attention. She looked up at me and I gasped -- I should not have seen her eyes in the dark -- they should have been dark indistinct spots on her face but I saw two golden pinpoints of light staring up at me.

My gasp startled the woman and the pinpoints of light vanished for a second as she continued to stare then they reappeared. I realized she had just blinked.

Movement further down the street drew both of our attention and again I saw a shadow … a slithering shadow. It looked like thick, black smoke but moved with a definite purpose. There were more than one of them and the black, smoky tendrils moved in several directions.

With a small, terrified cry, the woman disappeared into an alley two buildings away.

My eyes returned to the living smoke -- one of the tendrils was slowly making its way toward my building. My heart pounded in a comic strip beat -- I pictured my chest actually moving with the rhythm of my fear.

Suddenly, the heaviness in my limbs overwhelmed me. I turned and made my way, clumsily, through the dark apartment until I found and fell into my bed. With panic, I realized I was descending into the helplessness of unconsciousness and the shadows were coming to claim me …

I didn't know how long I floated blind but somewhere along the dark journey I became entwined with another body -- a female -- warm and soft. I let my hands tour her curves. A pair of breasts pressed against my chest. A mellifluous, feminine voice whispered my name.

"Richard …"

I felt a smile lift my features. I liked the way she spoke my name in the dark … so sensual …so urgent.

"Richard …"

God, I wanted her. I found the top of her head with my lips and kissed fragrant hair. I made my way to her mouth. She responded readily enough to my kisses. My hands were inexplicably clumsy as my caresses became more demanding. I cursed my own clumsiness. *Why was it so difficult to lift my arms?*

"Richard …"

I became lost in the frenzy of my own lust.

"Richard Shelton!"

With a jolt, I knew who the woman was. She clutched my shoulders in desperation, not passion.

"Ivey?"

"I can't stay here but I have to talk to you. Listen very carefully: we have to get out of Urbania before lights out tomorrow night." Her disembodied voice floated up from the general area of my throat.

"Why?" I asked. My tongue felt as heavy as my hands and I felt and sounded drunk. Am I dreaming all of this? "What about my Pulitzer?"

I felt her head move in a negative answer. "Forget that. It doesn't matter what Ketch told you. It isn't worth losing your life or … or worse. Trust me. Here, there are worse fates than death. Absorb what you can tomorrow but we must leave before the night is out. It won't take The Receivers long to figure out you're duping them …"

I wanted to ask a million questions at once but she silenced me with the sweetest of kisses. I tasted salt. Ivey was crying.

"I'll come for you tomorrow night and we'll leave this place … this beautiful, terrible place … this savage garden."

Then, she was gone and I was alone again in my blindness. I slept after that, I was certain of it.

I awoke in my bed. Pre-dawn light washed everything in the room with a blue hue. Ivey had returned and she watched me awaken from a corner. When she saw I was awake, she approached me, stripping off her gossamer robe as she came.

I was ready for her by the time she reached me. I didn't question why she had returned. I didn't question anything, I simply reacted. I made love to Ketch's woman. I took her because I wanted her, admired her and pitied her. When we were spent, I held her.

After a while, I looked around … the room was not familiar in the blue light … and yet it *was* familiar … a memory stirred and a chill swept over me. A deep fear clutched my gut but I couldn't understand quite what I was so frightened of.

I looked down at Ivey, who had been dozing peacefully in my arms, to find that she was staring up at me with her large, dark eyes. Without speaking a word, she ran her hands over me, light as down. Slowly, she rose above me and slipped one thigh over until she straddled my hips. She leaned down to kiss me. Her long, dark hair created a privacy curtain around our faces.

Between kisses, she said, "Tell me your dreams, Richard Shelton. Tell me your secrets. Why are you here?"

I was so lulled by the movement of her body that I couldn't think straight. "You know why I'm here …" I gasped.

"Tell me," she urged.

I looked into her eyes, her large, dark eyes … fathomless eyes … growing eyes. She leaned closer.

"Tell me, Richard. Why did you come here?" Her hips moved in punctuation of her words.

"You already know," I moaned in sweet torment. I could not tear my eyes from hers. She leaned down over me and her eyes grew large in her beautiful, tainted face.

There was something familiar about the moment but I could not put my finger on it. Her eyes drew me in and they continued to grow larger. My arousal left me as terror stirred.

Her eyes grew until they hideously distorted her face -- and still they continued to grow. I felt probing behind my own eyes as I stared into Ivey's ravenous, growing eyes. Her face drifted closer.

"Tell me … Richard Shelton … tell me everything …"

I awoke upright in bed, gasping as the nightmare reluctantly fled from me. I cried out and immediately grabbed my head. Sunlight poured into my room through the window, but I took no joy in it. The bright sunshine hurt my eyes. Damn pill. Ivey's drug had left me hung over and nauseous.

Slowly, I forced myself from the bed and I bathed in the efficient little bathroom. I felt human again by the time Shara arrived to take me to the market.

The marketplace turned out to be quite an experience. The set up took up most of about four city blocks, with merchants plying their wares beneath brightly colored tents. I found clothing and sandals. We gathered the items I would need to live comfortably. There was no payment that I could see, no currency exchanged hands for the items. Shara explained that Urbania's economy worked well at the retail level as a bartering system. Higher levels required currency and Urbania had its own form of currency.

I did not think I had anything of value to barter so I allowed Shara to handle my purchase negotiations. Finally, she turned to me. "Richard Shelton, this man has a vegetable farm." She indicated the merchant. "You will work there three days a week to pay for your clothes and you will also receive a portion of the vegetables. Is this a satisfactory arrangement?"

They both looked at me expectantly. A morning breeze ruffled the edges of Shara's lime green sari-like garment. I had never seen bartering so efficiently executed before. "Um … sure … that sounds fine," I stammered. A familiar twitch went through my fingers. I couldn't wait to write Urbania's story.

After Shara arranged for my new clothes to be delivered to my apartment, she began my tour and education of Urbania. Her step was light and sure-footed in slippers that matched her garment. The other citizens glanced at us with only the mildest curiosity. Everyone wore garments similar to ours. Generally, they went about the business of their day with the smooth rhythm of routine. Still, there was something that worried at the edges of my mind. Something about the citizens' demeanor struck me as odd.

Overall, I noticed that the Great City was a unique and harmonious blending of high tech (such as the lights at night, the automatic doors, the intricate irrigation system supporting the immense plant life, the strange appliances in my apartment, etc.) and simple, primitive living. Shara arranged for a horse-drawn carriage to take us for an extensive tour of the city which she assured me was too much too walk.

The buildings were beautiful; I noticed some new structures under construction were heavily draped. I pointed this out to Shara.

With a matter-of-fact flip of the horses' reins, she urged the carriage past the site. "Most of our major construction is done at night to keep down the risk of any errant satellite pictures revealing our engineering techniques."

Urbania guards her secrets, Ketch's voice haunted me again. I watched his lips twist in a phantom image from my memory … and those dirty nails as he twisted his hands together in that incessant, nervous gesture.

As we rolled along, I continued to watch the citizens of the Great City and realized, with a start, what it was about them that nagged at me so. Despite the harmony and apparent unity, the people conducted their daily business with a resignation that reminded me of oppressed societies. Yes, that was it. These people exuded the same humbled attitude I had seen in my travels as a journalist, of oppressed societies -- only the surroundings in Urbania were more idyllic.

The people seemed content, but not *happy*. I wondered about the generational differences from the first settlers of Urbania -- the famous international sociological experiment that took on a life of its own. Those first settlers volunteered for the project. The next generations were born into the Urbanian life and the city had evolved moved drastically from its original purpose.

Presently, we arrived at a long building with several wings that branched off from the main structure. "This is the Education Center," Shara explained as we climbed down out of the carriage. "This is where Urbania's offspring come to be educated. Here, they are allowed to explore and develop their individual talents before they are old enough for The Joining, when their consciousness becomes part of the Mindstream."

I was still not clear on what the "Mindstream" was, but I knew I didn't care for the imagery the term produced.

"How does one join the Mindstream?" I asked as we entered the Education Center.

"That's … " Shara's eyes became distant as she considered my question, " … complicated. I think it's best we wait to address that process. You're not ready for the Joining, anyway."

We walked past classrooms and I saw several curious students glance at me. I followed Shara into an administration wing of the building where I was introduced to a man named Trek. Trek was a large, very black fellow who moved with a grace so gravity-defying as to be amusing.

Shara put me between her and Trek. "Richard Shelton is a new citizen. He is a writer and he will be needing education in our ways and some testing of his talents before he is ready for the Joining."

Trek's voice matched his stature, a booming baritone that made my eardrums tremble. "I don't get many adults," Trek noted. "Be here tomorrow morning at first light. Don't be late." With that, he turned and glided away.

On our way back out of the building, a group of teenagers -- various ages -- quietly passed us. The kids were all dressed in green jumpsuits with a large letter "B" emblazoned on the front and back. The kids followed their teacher with downcast faces. I looked at Shara, "Breakers?"

With a sneer of distaste, she nodded. "Yes, this is generally where one finds the 'breakers.' They are misfits, the law breakers. They are forbidden to speak to anyone besides their teacher and are ostracized from the local social order until they are reformed and ready for the Joining." Shara added, "It's ironic that, Ivey, the woman you met yesterday at the bathhouse, used to be a Breaker counselor."

I felt my own brows lift. "Oh, really? What happened?"

Shara looked around and decided not to comment until she was outside. We climbed back into the carriage. Finally, she turned to me. "Ivey was, from what I was told, a great Breaker counselor with a high reform success rate. Her fatal mistake was when she had an affair with one of her students, an anarchist named, John Ketchum. She and Ketchum tried to escape … he was successful but she was caught. You've seen what her fate was." Shara shook her head, sadly. "It's a pity."

I was stunned. This news shed some new light on Ketch and his motive for helping me get into the Great City. I knew he wanted me to get Ivey out but now I understood the desperate urgency he must feel after having already failed her once.

Shara and I stopped for lunch at nearby café. The meal Shara ordered for us resembled Mediterranean fare and she ordered a smooth, sweet wine to accompany it. Near the end of our repast, a sound began somewhere behind me that sent a chill up my spine. It was soft at first, just a distracting noise in the background, but it rose in volume as the source drew nearer to us.

I realized it was the sound of footsteps on the tiled streets -- synchronized footsteps -- like a parade marching sequence. I turned in my seat to see a dozen identically clad, uniformed characters coming up the street toward us. They marched in an elaborate rhythm so perfect it seemed as if they were one entity. The percussion of their unified steps had a distinctive cadence. *Rat-tap-tap*.

They marched in double-file lines of six, looking straight ahead. Some male, some female – all wore dark glasses and androgynous haircuts. From Ketch's brief description (and his warnings), I knew who/what these people were even before I heard Shara softly announce, "Those are Transmitters."

I recalled Ketch's instructions if I should encounter Transmitters: *keep your mind blank. You must clear your mind.*

I tried to do just that and found it more difficult than I would have imagined. I gazed at my wine glass and focused on swirling the contents, nothing else but a focus on the swirling liquid and the way the light played upon glass and the wine.

When the footsteps were right beside us, I realized the other citizens around us quieted. Out of the corner of my eye, I saw 12 heads turn and all those eyes peered at me from behind dark glasses. I felt a very real sense of being probed from behind my eyes and the sensation horrified me.

I concentrated harder at staring at my wine glass and I focused every thought on that liquid.

Some images came to me, flashing superimposed over the wine: a dark-haired woman … screams and tears … I gritted my teeth. Beads of sweat broke out on my forehead. The probing became unbearably invasive. Something about it was far worse than the physical violation I endured the day before.

The glass, the curved sides and the unusual color of the wine -- a deep, orange hue … I wondered what fruit had been used to create it.

Finally, the probing ceased and the eyes turned away. The Transmitters passed by. Gradually, the citizens around us came alive again.

Shara and I finished our meal in relative silence. Afterward, she continued my tour of Urbania, and it seemed the wonders of the Great City never ceased. Our carriage carried us to a place where the larger buildings thinned and the foliage increased until we were traveling in a forest, which opened up to vast farmlands and orchards -- miles of them. Shara eventually brought the carriage to a halt in a clearing at the edge of an enormous lake. I couldn't fathom it. We were supposed to be in the Nevada desert.

"How was this done?"

Shara smiled as she gazed out over the water. "There is nothing that can't be done when great minds unite. I brought you here to show you what you have become a part of -- what you will contribute to."

Shara's profile faded before my eyes as a vision took hold …

… a dark-haired woman … and a monster. I shivered as something tried to take hold of me. I had a premonition of myself looking into a mirror. My own reflection gleamed back at me and my eyes held golden pinpoints of light where the pupils should be.

I snapped back to the present with a gasp. Shara stared at me with a bemused expression. "What just happened to you?"

I told her about what I experienced. She nodded in understanding. "The Mindstream is reaching for you. Don't fight it."

I looked out in the distance, across the lake, and wondered at the distant line of clouds on the horizon until I realized I was not seeing clouds.

It was the wall -- Urbania's physical boundary. I jerked as another vision took me.

I stood in front of a mirror and a chill wriggled its way under my skin as I realized someone stood behind me, at my right shoulder. I saw and recognized Nestor's cold smile. He stood very close. I could feel his steady breath on the back of my neck. Our eyes met in the mirror. I felt the probe again -- inside my head -- and with it I discovered an irresistible urge to fight it. The pupils of Nestor's eyes began glowing with the golden light.

"Who are you? Why are you here?" He pressed. His cold, knowing smile brought out a fear that sickened me. I could not name my distress except to say it brought me a vague but deep anxiety.

I tore my eyes from his and looked into my own for answers. A pair of golden lights winked on in my eyes and the probing intensified … the image dissolved into another vision of the dark-haired woman … as usual, I could not see her face. She was surrounded by people. I heard her screams as hands held her down.

The vision shifted again and Nestor stood before me and transformed into a black shadow … a living shadow with golden lights for eyes … and an open mouth. He reared back like a cobra. I cried out and raised my arms instinctively in defense. The shadow's mouth opened wider and clamped down on my arm.

I screamed as my arm disappeared into the shadow's maw …

"Richard!"

The sound of my name being called with such urgency snatched me from the vision's clutches and I was back with Shara. Sunlight glinted off her diamond-studded scalp. She looked frightened as she reached for me but I had scooted too far across the carriage seat and suddenly my arms spun at air as I toppled backwards off the carriage. I hit the ground with an awful *thud*.

Shara leapt from the transport to come to my aid. I panicked as I could not seem to get a breath. Finally, I inhaled and a long, pained moan escaped me. Gradually, we assessed no real damage.

"What happened?" Shara asked.

I told her about the new vision and asked what the golden lights were.

"Oh, that's the pulsing of the Mindstream. It means the Mindstream is in direct contact," she explained.

I remembered the shadow's bite and raised the sleeve of my tunic and found a half-moon shaped bruise forming.

Shara looked upset. "I don't understand this. The Mindstream is run by the Transmitters and the Receivers … they can't cause this kind of physical harm."

I jerked my arm away from her and stood shakily. Hands on my hips, I surveyed the beautiful scenery around me. "Tell me something, Shara. Urbania has discovered how to gain water and grow plants in a desert. I know you have immense weapons that we could not begin to understand in The World -- we saw evidence of that when Urbania shot down the spy satellites all those years ago and withdrew from the rest of the world. I'm sure you've cured diseases and created masterful works of art."

Shara grew impatient. I felt she caught the drift of where I was headed and she was not happy about it. I shook up her little world with my observations.

"What is your question, Richard?"

"Why won't you share all these wonders with the rest of humanity? Isn't that what the Urbanian Social Project was originally intended to do? You've broken down centuries of carefully constructed civilization. What have you replaced it with? To what end?"

"The Great City is still evolving, Richard. We are our own entity and we are so far removed and above The World that we see no point in wasting our knowledge on a world that would only exploit it."

Golden lights began to glow in Shara's eyes and I wondered who really answered me -- Shara or the manipulators of the Mindstream.

"Do you really think the rest of the world would benefit? Or, do you know -- as we do -- that our precious gifts of knowledge would end up tainted and horded by the powerful and misery would never really be alleviated?" Shara asked.

I pondered this as Shara helped me climb back into the carriage. A question, a line from Ayn Rand's novel, *Atlas Shrugged*, 'who is John Galt?' ... A man who said he would stop man's machinery and did. I sighed and murmured that question aloud as I settled into my seat.

Shara surprised me with a twinkling laugh. "Ayn Rand. Yes, *Atlas Shrugged*, how appropriate."

"You know of her work?"

Shara turned to me with a look that was almost sinister. A spidery chill scurried up my spine. "Yes, of course. Her work and her ideals made her a literary legend. However, here in The Great City, we prefer not to stand on the shoulders of giants, but to create giants of our own."

With that, Shara urged the horses into motion and we turned back toward the city.

That evening, just before sunset, Shara and I shared a meal in my apartment. She prepared it and showed me how to use the strange-looking stove. She finally left me alone with a reminder about my classes to begin in the morning.

Later, I stood alone on my balcony and watched as the lights came on in a wash of color and brightness. I sighed with wonder.

"Don't be deceived by all the beauty. Urbania's draw is not equal to her demands."

I whirled around. Ivey hovered just behind me near the patio doorway. She tried not to be seen by any passersby below or any neighboring apartments. She backed into the apartment and I followed her, drawing a set of light, fabric curtains closed behind me. A light breeze gently stirred the curtains but left us our privacy.

I'm beginning to understand what you mean," I said.

Like a wraith, she drifted around the couches of my living room and finally settled in the corner of one, curling a leg beneath her as she sat down. "You understand nothing, Richard. You would have to live here to truly know what an independent mind goes through.

"The Mindstream is an abomination. People should able to own their own damn thoughts! Everyone should be allowed at least that much privacy."

I watched a myriad of emotions play across her face. She seemed to fight tears -- a drowning pool of them.

I posed a question that had been worrying at me like a cat toys with its prey. "What are the Receivers?"

Diverted from tears, her eyes immediately locked onto mine. I read a hint of fear and surprise in those dark depths.

"Can't you tell," she asked. "Isn't it obvious?"

The answer stirred within me but wouldn't rear up enough for me to catch hold and pull it into the light of understanding. *Damn, I wish I had my pen and paper. I think better that way.*

Ivey rose from the couch and drifted toward me. "We cannot linger, Richard. There's so much about the Great City that you could not ever conceive of. You could not begin to comprehend the creations that have been wrought here."

"I want to know," I whispered. My voice sounded hoarse to my ears. My body was very much aware of Ivey's nearness. A strange sense of power emanated from her and I found it seductive.

Ivey closed the distance between us. I felt the warmth of her skin just a touch away from mine. I held my breath as she spoke. "This city is teeming with life, Richard. We all interact."

She raised her palms, facing outward, just slightly. With a slight smile she began to whisper in a jumble of soft sounds that held the rhythm and cadence of language.

After a moment, it seemed everything in the room was held in her thrall. It almost seemed as if even the couches were leaning in. I looked over at my curtains to find them frozen inward, pointing toward Ivey. The fine hairs on my arms stood on end and leaned in her direction, as if magnetized.

A grunt in her throat broke the spell. The curtains fell back into the hand of the breeze that played with them again. The hairs on my arms settled back into place.

I looked into Ivey's eyes. "You're not plugged into the Mindstream are you?"

"I used to be. I was a loyal acolyte of Urbania until I found out what they wanted from Ketch … what they wanted to do to him. I also saw what they did to one of my other students. They raped his mind while I watched. They broke him and turned him into a Transmitter."

"I don't see any golden light in your eyes. How have you avoided the Mindstream?"

Ivey's gaze went through me. "Ketch taught me. He taught me how to protect myself. Ketch taught me a lot of things." Her eyes were so sad and melancholy.

Without thinking, I slid my arms around her. She stiffened at first -- I don't know if I surprised her. Then, as if making a decision, she sighed softly and allowed herself to melt into my embrace. I kissed her hair and gently kissed the ugly, puckered "B" on her forehead.

"It feels so good to be touched," she whispered and my heart seized for a second in a moment of intense sympathy for what this woman had endured. She must be starved for contact, for love. I ran my hands along her back, down to her waist, where I gripped her and pulled her tight against me.

She lifted her face toward me and I lowered my mouth to hers for a kiss. Within that kiss, I swallowed her moans and deepened it so that I could taste her.

With great care, I removed the gossamer robes she wore and I touched every silky inch of her. She reveled in the contact and, in return, she feasted on my skin with her fingertips as she helped me loosen and remove my tunic and pants. We drifted down the hall to my bedroom where we continued our love-play on my bed.

I freed her dark hair from the simple braid she kept it in and the multi-colored lights from outside the window poured over her body and painted her as a goddess that I worshiped with my hands and lips. She whimpered in increased urgency and pleasure as I accustomed the cup of my hand to the curve of her breast.

The urgency of passion increased until I rolled her onto her back and moved between her parted thighs. I poised to enter her but she suddenly grasped my hips to stop me.

She rose up and nipped at my bottom lip then raised put her lips close to my ear and whispered, "You realize that this act does not make me yours. My heart belongs to Ketch."

I was too far gone to care precisely what she meant by that. "How unfortunate for you that he is not here. You have me instead," I said as I entered her with one smooth thrust. A deep moan issued from her throat and anything else that might have been said between us was forgotten.

Later, I woke next to Ivey. It was dark … I didn't understand the significance of this until Ivey woke moments later. "Shit! It's past lights out! The Receivers will be coming. We've got to go, NOW!"

We scrambled from the bed and dressed.

"Where are we going?" I asked as we fumbled through my dark apartment.

"To the wall on the south side of the city … near the gate."

"But, what about the sentinels?" I thought about Nestor and shuddered.

"The Sentinels are the least of our worries."

I opened my mouth to inflict another question upon her but she silenced me with an abrupt movement of her hand. As quietly as possible, we made it down hallways and two flights of stairs until we reached the ground floor. I was stunned by darkness once we stepped outside the building. What little moonlight penetrated above the street was snuffed out by the shadow of the buildings looming around us.

Our sandals made barely a whisper of sound on the tiled streets as we melded with shadows and quickly moved toward the city's entrance. Ivey's fear was apparent and contagious, perhaps because she was more aware of what we faced if we were caught. A vision flashed in my mind, blinding me for a few seconds. I saw a dark-haired woman, screaming as she was dragged through Urbania's streets -- friction tearing her clothing away.

The vision ended and I was left trembling. I almost yelped when Ivey's hand clamped onto my forearm. I had slowed down and she drew me along faster to match her pace. Between buildings, a sliver of moonlight revealed our surroundings. I glanced down at my shadow … and I went very still.

"Ivey." My voice held a wavering note of fear. With her hand still holding my arm in a death grip, Ivey skidded to a stop when I stopped.

After a brief, impatient snort, she examined my features more closely in the dimness. "What's wrong, Richard?"

Quite suddenly, I found I was too frightened to speak. My tongue felt thick and dry. I stared down at my shadow, where it sprouted out to the left of my feet. Then, I glanced to my right to see my shadow … again.

"Look!" I hissed as I pointed at Ivey's feet. She also sported dual shadows. I glanced up to check the moon's angle. I wanted to know which shadow was the imposter.

I decided the shadow on my left was the imposter and as I watched, the image grew blacker.

In my growing terror, my limbs felt shaky and unstable. I heard Ivey whisper, 'What made me think we could fool them?" Her voice sounded younger -- vulnerable -- and I didn't like it.

"Ivey?"

She didn't answer me. She stared at the dual shadows. When she didn't respond and I took her by her shoulders. "Ivey. What is it?"

She raised enormous black eyes to me. "Receivers."

I looked down to see the imposter shadows writhe and rise. They came to full height -- a life-sized mirror in front of me -- a pair of golden eyes opened and looked into mine. I looked away as I grabbed Ivey's arm and screamed, "Ruuuuuuuunnnnnnn!"

This appeared to break through her shock and she came to life with jolt and she began to run with me. We no longer made any attempt to be silent as our sandals slapped the street. I glanced behind to see the shadow beings become smoke, joined by other tendrils, and they flowed toward us in a vaporous black tidal wave with hundreds of glittering, golden eyes.

The slapping of our sandals on the street was joined by the sound of synchronized tapping as packs of Transmitters -- dozens of them -- flowed from the side streets. In one instant, just before we reached the wall, I managed a good, long look at one of the shadow beings and suddenly I realized in horror what they were.

Can't you tell? Isn't it obvious? Ivey's comment back in my apartment earlier came back to haunt me. Human. They were no longer human as I would understand it, but they were human at one time. Watching their movements and interactions, I sensed the truth.

I followed Ivey behind a thick stand of trees and bushes and I realized we reached the wall. She felt along the bricks until she came to a particular spot where she tugged violently until a small, hidden door opened. From within the secret hiding place, she removed a long cord, a grappling hook and a large old-fashioned gun.

We were hidden behind some enormous flowering trees but I heard the footsteps of the Transmitters all around us. I found a strange comfort in the sound of their steps. I could at least discern their locations. I worried more about the Receivers and found myself jumping at every shadow.

"Stand back," Ivey hissed as she tried to load the hook into the gun and dropped the hook. Then she had trouble getting the hook to load properly. "Shit! I can do this … I've practiced it over and over in my mind," she whispered. She finally loaded the gun with shaking hands and launched the hook.

I held my breath as the hook caught on the top of the wall. She tested it and it held.

"Climb, Richard!" she ordered.

I took one look at the height. "You first."

She would have none of it. She took the thick cord and one of my hands. Her voice became an impatient hiss. "*Climb.*"

I stood my ground. "You *first.*"

I felt her glare, even through the veil of darkness. "I can take care of myself, trust me. Now, I will say it one more time – you will *climb!*"

I climbed.

Halfway up the wall, my arms screamed in protest as I rose past the tops of trees. I felt them before I saw them -- the Receivers. A chill along my spine cause me to shudder and I almost lost my grip on the rope. Looking down was like glancing into a dark well. I saw a pale oval that was Ivey's face and I saw a river of blackness flowing toward her and I heard the sound of hundreds of synchronized footsteps drawing closer.

"Ivey," I whispered.

"Keep climbing!" Ivey screamed into the privacy of my thoughts. I gasped at the sensation -- it was like being jabbed from the inside. I continued my ascent until I reached the top of the wall. There was a wide walkway along the top and I was able to stand and look back down at Ivey.

She was not on the rope. Through tree branches and darkness, I could only catch glimpses of her. I could hear sounds of struggling below. I heard Ivey scream once and I called her name. The wind picked up and the tree tops bounced and swayed, leaves swished together.

I screamed Ivey's name down into the murky unknown. I leaned dangerously far out over the edge. I was prepared to go back down if needed, much as the thought sickened me with fear.

A woman's voice next to me nearly sent me sailing out over the edge. I jerked my head to see who spoke my name and found Ivey next to me. "Let's go, Richard."

Her hand descended on my shoulder. "How did you get up here?" I asked, breathless.

A hundred voices below simultaneously accused, "Illegal use of will!"

Moonlight glinted off tears in Ivey's eyes.

Hundreds of hooks sailed above our heads and we dodged ropes as Transmitters prepared to scale the wall in pursuit.

"What happened in this city?" I asked as Ivey pulled me to a shaky stand.

"Evil geniuses and a bad enchantment," she said in an emotionally choked sob.

The Transmitters' footsteps *clacked* along the brick wall -- not quite as synchronized as on the ground. I grabbed my rope and prepared to go down the other side of the wall. Ivey stopped me.

"Put your arms around me, Richard. I've got a faster way and we don't have much to lose now."

For once, I did not argue. We held each other in a tight embrace. Ivey's breathing increased to a near pant and the wind increased in tempo with her breathing. I felt the press of … something … all around us. It crowded our atmosphere and weighted my chest -- making each breath a burden. Then, we were lifted up and carried out over the edge of the wall. I held Ivey tight as we were lowered and set safely down on sacred ground outside of Urbania's wall. I wanted to fall and kiss it if I had not been so overcome by what Ivey had just done.

I heard a lot of noise and when I looked up I saw a line of Transmitters had topped the wall. *That's not nearly all of them*, I thought, briefly. Ivey and I instinctively reached for each other's hand as we ran. An enormous sound ahead of us halted us in our tracks.

Urbania's gate rumbled and clanked along its track as it opened.

The thump of feet behind us told me that at least 100 Transmitters or more had managed to come over the wall. Armed sentinels and immense clusters of Transmitters began to pour out from the gate, even as it was still opening. I took note of the fact that the Transmitters could be divided to different duties at the same time. This seemed important, somehow.

Transmitters behind us and Transmitters and sentinels ahead of us … and Receivers coming toward the gate like a tidal wave of tar. However, as the wave reached the entrance to the city, it began to thin and break apart like a dog that reached the end of its chain. The Receiver wave pulled back and waited -- a malevolent cloud of golden eyes -- at a distance.

Beside me, Ivey barked a harsh laugh. "So, it's true … the Receivers can't leave the boundaries of the Great City. Their source of power, of cohesion, is the Mindstream."

"The Transmitters are different, though." I noted. She nodded, absently.

We were surrounded and we knew it. Nestor approached with his weapon trained on us. I realized there were far more Transmitters than sentinels.

"Be prepared to run on my signal," Ivey said, low.

"They'll kill us …" I mumbled from a dry throat. My lower abdomen burned with fear.

"Death is better than what they will do to you -- do you want to be like them?" She indicated the Transmitters with a subtle thrust of her chin.

I studied them a moment before resigning myself to my fate. I sighed. "No, I don't want to be one of them."

She turned to me suddenly with a brilliant smile. "Don't worry, no one will die tonight. He's coming, I can feel him … and no one will be left behind this time."

I touched her face but found no words. She seemed to understand.

A sound rose in the hot desert night, a familiar sound … I realized, with wonder, it was a car. I looked and saw a dust cloud making its way toward us at high speed. I glanced back and saw the sentinels had trained their guns on it.

Like a specter from the darkness, a car tore down the desert highway and screeched to a stop in front of Urbania's gate. A strange, muffled cry from Ivey told me who it was even before Ketch got out of the driver's seat and walked around.

Nestor sneered. "So, Urbania's own prodigal son returns."

"Nope," said Ketch. "I'm just stopping by."

A hush fell. The Transmitters inched closer, the sentinels shouldered their weapons and prepared to fire and the Receivers were a swirling, agitated mass roiling just inside the gate like a witch's brew.

Nestor laughed. "What audacity! Do you really think we will let you leave now that you're back within our grasp?"

Ketch's smile was slow, deliberate and cold. "What makes you think you can stop me?"

As soon as Ketch's words were spoken, I sensed a change in the air. The Transmitters began a painful screeching -- they grabbed their heads and half of them were on their knees. The sentinels dropped their weapons and looked dazed and confused.

The Receivers shrank further back and began to separate and dispense like smoke in the wind. Nestor wept like a child, but his look was murderous. "What are you *doing*?"

"The Mindstream is your power. Mark my words, Nestor, it will one day be the very thing that brings the Great City down."

Ketch signaled for Ivey and me to come. Ivey ran to him and threw herself into his arms. I felt a terrible spasm in my heart. I had fallen in love with a woman in love.

Ketch tossed me the keys to the car, which I now realized, was a souped-up antique --an impressive antique – a 1965, Ford Galaxy 500, convertible. The car had been lovingly restored. With a start, I recalled all the times I'd noticed the oddity of Ketch's dirty nails and wondered at where a recluse had gotten so dirty. Now, I knew.

"Drive," he said.

I drove.

Ketch and Ivey had an emotional reunion in the backseat. I tried not to intrude but some masochistic, love-sick instinct repeatedly pulled my eyes to the rearview mirror. I watched Ketch and Ivey as they touched each other's faces -- both of them crying. I also watched the moment Ketch, with exquisite tenderness, traced the puckered scar on Ivey's forehead with his fingers.

"They will pay for this," he murmured through gritted teeth, "I will reveal their secrets to the world and I will tear down their carefully constructed walls!"

A strength emanated from Ketch like I'd never seen before. I had thought him to be lost and broken, but that was before he had Ivey back.

After a while, Ketch ordered me to pull over. He and Ivey got into the front and I climbed into the back. Ketch reached in the floor by Ivey's feet and picked up a shopping bag I hadn't noticed before. He tossed it back to me. "Do what you've been itching to do, Shelton. Do what you were born to do … *write*."

I peered into the bag and found six spiral-bound notebooks and a package of pens.

The next several hours were a blur of words I wrote in a frenzied orgy of thoughts, memories and observations from my brief time in Urbania. At times, I would come out of myself to hear Ivey and Ketch murmuring softly to each other or I would stare out into the blackness of the desert highway outside the car's windows. The stars were the only measure of what separated earth and sky.

There were many moments from that dramatic escape and the trip afterward that I etched forever into my memory but nothing shook me to my soul more than the image of Ivey laughing into the orange/pink dawn.

I looked up from my notebooks at the sound of Ivey's gasp and I saw her pointing to the East, where we were headed. She stared at the birth of a new day and she begged Ketch to put the top down on the convertible. He obliged and I grabbed my notebooks against the sudden onslaught of wind. Ivey stood up in her seat and hung onto the windshield for support.

She laughed like a child at the growing beauty of the orange-fade-to-brilliant pink dawn. She pointed at it again and looked down at Ketch and me and she yelled above roaring wind, "*That* is the color of victory … the color of hope!"

She looked at the dawn again and I didn't think I had ever seen anything more fiercely beautiful than dawn's light on Ivey's face as she smiled into the morning -- tears streaking back from her eyes and her long, dark hair blowing in the wind.

It struck me suddenly that Ivey was a child of the Great City, just like Ketch. They were born there. She had never been outside of Urbania. I could not begin to imagine how she felt as she embraced a new dawn as a free woman.

We drove all day and into the night and arrived at Ketch's apartment the second dawn. We took turns sleeping and driving. We all slept -- Ivey and Ketch shared his bedroom and I slept on the couch with Ketch's cats curled up around me. I thought I'd find it annoying but all the warm, furry bodies comforted me instead and kept the bad dreams away … until later in the afternoon when I was in the shower.

I stood beneath the warm spray and was taken suddenly and violently by a vision … the woman … the creatures … the terror.

I must have been screaming because Ivey and Ketch were with me when my vision cleared. Ketch was in the shower with me fully dressed and completely soaked. We were crouched down in the tub. Ivey stood near the tiny sink, next to the bathroom door, which had obviously been kicked in.

"What happened, Richard? Are you all right? What did you see? Was it the visions again?" Ketch rapid-fired worried questions at me when he saw I was lucid again.

My eyes felt huge in my head as I looked at him. "Not a vision … they are not visions … are they? When I see these images, they are not visions. They are memories, aren't they? I've been there before."

Ketch's expression was solemn and pale. "Yes, Richard. They're memories. I'll tell you what I know. I think you're ready but first we have to get some clothes on you and I've got to get dry."

He turned off the shower and helped me from the tub. I stood on shaky legs as Ivey dried me. Ketch peeled off his wet clothes and grabbed a towel to dry himself. I realized I found so many of Ketch's movements to be familiar and I wondered at this.

I also realized I felt no shame being naked in front of either one of them. Ivey led me into Ketch's bedroom and picked out some clothes for me. Ketch and I were roughly the same size. Her eyes met mine one time. She gave me a warm and reassuring smile. With sadness, I realized the night I'd spent in her arms was the only one I would ever have and now it seemed eons ago -- almost like it didn't happen.

"It happened, Richard. It happened because we both needed it to happen but I don't belong with you," Ivey said in a low voice. Once again, she startled me by reading my thoughts.

"If you don't like it then shield your thoughts better," she said with a chuckle.

Ketch came into the room, naked, and plucked some clothes from his battered chest-of-drawers. He began to speak in a weary and strangely emotional voice.

"Why did you find me, Richard? Why did you want to see Urbania so badly?"

Feeling weak, I sat down on the edge of the unmade bed. I detected the lingering scent of love making. It appeared Ketch and Ivey had picked up where they left off. I wracked my battered brain for details. "I found you through an informant. Urbania was a hobby of mine since childhood. The place has been a mystery for so long. I have always been obsessed with it … with uncovering its secrets and with discovering the truth. Truth has been the only thing that mattered to me."

Ketch moved to me and knelt at my feet. "What about your childhood? What do you remember of that?"

"I don't like to talk about my childhood." I felt a muscle in my jaw tense.

"Why?" He pressed.

"Because I didn't really have one that I know of," I admitted in a raw voice.

Ivey came to sit on the bed next to me. She gently touched my shoulder. "Tell us, Richard."

I laughed self-consciously. "There's not much to tell. I was an orphan. I grew up in a private children's home in Las Vegas. I lived there from about the age of fourteen."

Ketch made a strange sound in his throat before he managed to speak again. "And, before that?"

I looked into Ketch's eyes and realized I had never done that before. I had looked at his face but never directly into his eyes. I stared into a pair of intense, green eyes that pleaded with me to confess things I had told no one before. I don't know why, but I trusted the man kneeling before me. I trusted him and found a strong, almost childish, desire to confide in him. "Before that," I continued, "there's nothing -- absolutely nothing. I was found wandering the streets of Las Vegas and picked up by the police. I had no memory of who I was … or where I was from … nothing. It's like I didn't exist before the moment the cops found me.

"The doctors said I had gone through some kind of severe trauma that my mind had blocked out to protect me. I'm inclined to believe them. The only consistent thing my mind managed to conjure up were the dreams … and my obsession with the Great City. I've always been overly curious about Urbania. And, at the time I was found, there was a lot going on with it … Urbania had long finished the wall that surrounds it and they were murdering supplicants before the city gates. And it was about that time that the city destroyed the satellites trained on it after the United States government refused to stop spying," I stifled an involuntary, helpless gesture of my hands as I spoke.

"Because of Las Vegas' relatively close proximity to Urbania, I fantasized that I was from there and maybe I would learn its secrets and find myself in the process. Later, I realized that was a stupid, childhood dream. I mean, who doesn't want to be special? Right? But, as an adult … it all came down to truth. The truth is all that matters. I hate mystery. I've got too many of them in my own past and, as a journalist, Urbania was going to be my biggest accomplishment -- the biggest mystery to be uncovered before the world."

A heavy quiet settled on the room like a blanket. Ketch looked away from me and shared a meaningful glance with Ivey. "Tell him about Lucas," Ivey said.

"Lucas?" I looked from Ketch to Ivey and back.

Ketch cleared his throat and sat down flat on the floor and leaned his arms on his bent knees. He studied his arms for a long moment before he finally began to speak. "I had a little brother back in Urbania. His name was Lucas. He was four years younger than me. Lucas and I … well, we were all each other had. Our father was murdered by the Urbanian hierarchy -- although it was never proven -- and our mother died not long after that. Father was trying to uncover the aberrant twists Urbania had taken with the Mindstream -- that the Mindstream was not being used as a wondrous tool for an artistic and creative communion of minds. Instead, it was being used as a means of enslavement and mental robbery.

"The World -- as the Great City likes to sneer -- was still loosely connected to us then … although the bond was tenuous at best. The UN had created the project as a tool of peace and enlightenment between all the countries that participated in this social experiment. Well, you know what eventually happened. Father was going to attempt to let the outside world know what was going on … maybe get some help before Urbania isolated itself completely. He knew where it was going … he saw it coming and knew the immense weaponry Urbania had at its disposal. These are weapons no one would guess could exist. There are some frightening things that can come about when great minds come together."

Ketch shifted slightly. I leaned forward, anxious and sensing he had not yet told me what he wanted me to know.

"I was nearly eighteen when Father was murdered," Ketch continued. "I tried to continue what he was doing … to get The World involved. My brother, Lucas, was young, grieving and helpless and I was bitter … and on a mission. When I turned eighteen shortly after my father's death, I went through some standard "gift" testing at the Education Center and it turned up some interesting facts.

"These were things that Father had already suspected … he was a great scientist … and my mother was an artist who possessed some strong psychic tendencies. I possessed all of that and more … I was something different in that I could 'control' the Mindstream instead of the other way around. I could also hide my thoughts from it, even when sleeping -- a highly illegal practice known as 'caching.' I was a potential threat and the Receivers wanted me badly … badly enough to do anything to turn me into a lab rat. I was termed a 'Breaker,' and placed into Ivey's group for reforming."

Ketch paused for a moment to smile gently at Ivey. She picked up the story for a moment. "Ketch came to me as one of my students and I knew he was rather old for reform. I was a strong believer in the Urbanian way of life. I was a patriot, as it were. I had some psychic abilities of my own that I suppressed because of Urbanian law. When I saw that the 'crimes' Ketch was accused of, the ones that sentenced him to 'Breaker' status, I felt that his punishment seemed far too great. That was what got me to finally taking a look at what was going on in the Great City. Then, I got to see Ketch's test results and it didn't take long for me to see the real reason he was being held."

Ketch nodded. "You know that Ivey and I got together and made an escape attempt. She had no one to leave behind but I had Lucas. I wanted to take him with me. I didn't want him to suffer for my crimes. Plus, he had not been tested yet and I worried at what they would find in him, as well. The night that Ivey and I planned our escape, we tried to take Lucas with us but he didn't understand … didn't believe us and he refused to come at first but Ivey convinced him.

"He got scared when the Receivers and the Transmitters were in pursuit … he got scared and … surrendered. Ivey stopped to help him … and there was a split second where it was apparent that we were not going to make it out … and she made me go. She said she would stay with Lucas and she made me go." Ketch's voice caught. I watched him fight tears. He could not continue.

Ivey finished it for him, "I had to do it. If any of us got out, it had to be Ketch. He was the one that the Receivers really wanted … and he was the one with the power to truly harm the Great City. If they caught Ketch, then we were all dead or worse. If he got away then Lucas and I would have a chance. I convinced Ketch to run. I helped him over the wall … and then I held Lucas in my arms as we were captured.

"When the Transmitters attempted to take Lucas, he finally fought. He fought hard. He fought because he was trying to stop them from hurting me. I was dragged by my feet through the streets until the friction stripped away my clothes … I was drug naked until my skin was bleeding and abraded. I was beaten … mentally tortured … and finally … physically branded in the center of the city. Nestor had me held down while he affixed the brand himself. Lucas saw the whole thing … poor, poor kid." Ivey stopped. She was crying she slid onto the floor and crawled into Ketch's waiting arms and they held each other like children.

I felt tears sliding down my own face. "What happened to Lucas?"

Ivey answered after a moment to compose herself. "He disappeared. One night the city's alarm was raised and there was a terrible ruckus … I learned later that Lucas escaped. I told this to Ketch."

"You told Ketch? How?"

Ivey managed a smile and she turned to look into Ketch's eyes as she spoke. "Ketch and I have discovered a bond … we can speak to each other no matter where we are … anytime …."

"Oh."

Ketch finished the tale, "I searched for Lucas. It was difficult but after weeks of searching, I found a police report about a kid about Lucas's age being found in Las Vegas. I went there and … I learned of the kid's condition and I knew my brother when I saw him. I kept an eye on him from a distance … and I knew … I knew someday … I would have him back but he was safer where he was at that time. I didn't want to cause him any damage but I watched him … learned of his proclivities … including an obsession with Urbania. An obsession he didn't understand … I fed that obsession … I sent an informant that finally led him to me."

Stunned, I stared at Ketch and Ivey until Ketch's words saturated my consciousness like water into a sponge. "Not visions … memories …"

Ketch smiled, "Yes, Lucas … memories. Now, you have uncovered the one mystery you never thought you would. You now know who you are."

"Why didn't you just tell me?"

Ketch and Ivey separated and Ketch got to his feet and approached me. He took my arm and gently tugged me to my feet. "Like I said, you were damaged – severely traumatized. I didn't want to cause you any further harm, but the things you told me about your visions … the things that convinced me that you needed to go to Urbania … well, I knew that day would come. I knew that you could get into the city, learn enough of its secrets to expose it to the world and help me get Ivey back. I could not have gotten her out without help. I would have risked anything to get her out except being captured."

Ivey rose to her feet. "Ketch being captured was not, and can never be, an option. We think he could possibly have rescued me on his own but we couldn't risk it. His powers can never be used for the Mindstream. That would put the whole world in danger -- not just Urbanians."

I felt a frown pucker my brow as I considered what Ivey said. "He's that powerful? His gifts are potentially that dangerous?"

"Without a doubt," she said, firmly. "As long as Ketch stays in control of his gifts, we can use them to bring Urbania down … what worried me when you came along is that you, being his brother, might have had the same potential. It really is amazing that the Mindstream didn't learn about who you really are while you were there. So, I can only think that you may have latent gifts similar to Ketch's.

"Your amnesia was also a blessing for that situation. Still … I felt your mind working to repair itself … working to rediscover what you had lost. We were lucky to escape when we did. Ketch has developed his gifts enough now that we think he could fight off the Mindstream but even he is not invulnerable. You would have been a prime candidate for Head Lab Rat if we had stayed any longer."

Remembering the Transmitters and the Receivers, I shuddered.

My stomach chose that moment to growl. We all laughed.

"Biology has its own timetable. Let's get something to eat. There's a great Italian place just around the corner. I'll get us some take-out," suggested Ketch.

Within an hour, we were eating ravioli, manicotti and lasagna and laughing at Ketch's jokes. I had a moment, a good moment, of belonging. I could not recall a time when I had felt that. I looked at the late afternoon sunshine pouring through two dirty windows, lighting Ketch's apartment.

I was warmed by Ivey's smile as she tried Italian food for the first time. Her eyes slid closed in an almost orgasmic reaction. Ketch grinned at her and dabbed sauce from her chin with a paper towel. We toasted with good Chianti. The moment was one frozen in time -- a good, forever moment. I locked it inside me for safekeeping.

The moment was so sacred to me that I didn't want let it go, even when I began to feel strange. My head began to ache … a crawly sensation reminiscent of my time in Urbania. I could hide my discomfort no longer when the visions began … something in my memory stirred … and it awakened with a powerful jolt … suddenly it became clear … my mind cleared like a fog blowing away after sunrise. I jumped up from the table with a scream, knocking my chair over. I grabbed my head. "No, no, no, NOOOOOOOOOOOOOO! Get out! Get out!!"

Ketch and Ivey came to me, both looking frightened. I heard them and felt their hands on me but my eyes were squeezed tightly shut. I cried -- great, wrenching sobs. I tried to tell them what was wrong over the din that filled my head.

"Memories … not visions! I didn't escape Urbania … I didn't escape!!"

"What do you mean, Lucas? I don't know what you're –" Ketch's words died in his throat as I opened my eyes.

"Oh, my god!" Ivey screamed as she backed away from me. I glanced at Ketch's blank television screen and it reflected what they saw. Golden lights pulsed within my eyes.

"No!" I struggled against what was happening to me. The cocoon that had swathed my brain for so many years unraveled and my life was handed back to me in one swoop. I tried to tell them what they needed to know … I knew we didn't have long before … before … I struggled to tell them. "No escape! I didn't escape … was … captured … was … programmed and released …no choice … a sleeper!"

My head swam and ached. I turned and violently vomited what I had eaten onto Ketch's kitchen floor. I cried and choked while I puked. Afterward, I wiped my mouth on my sleeve.

"Lucas, what are you saying?" Ketch asked, desperately. He held Ivey, who trembled and shook as she stared at me with her huge, dark eyes. I wanted to reassure her but didn't dare try to touch her in her near-panicked state.

"You don't have much time!" I managed to gasp.

"What –" Ketch was cut off when Ivey raised a hand to silence him. Her head was cocked to one side, listening.

"What's that? I hear … something …"

"The Receivers can't travel outside of Urbania's gates," I began, "but the Transmitters can."

Softly, somewhere within the building … we could hear a sound. A sound that grew. It was the sound of synchronized footsteps marching at a steady, deadly cadence.

"No, no, no … I won't go back! I won't go back there!"

My throat was low, gravely from my violent vomiting episode. "You two must get out! Run! Leave here. They're following me! It was me that led them here. I didn't know … I couldn't help it ….I'm a new weapon -- a new kind of Transmitter." I stumbled to the grocery bag that held my notebooks. I picked it up and tossed it to Ketch. He caught it nimbly. I gave him what I hoped was a tender smile. I hoped he knew how I felt.

"My notes are complete. Get them to my editor … truth and love is all that matters. It's all we have to fight with. Bring those bastards *down*, brother." I felt my mind, my will and my body weakening beneath the onslaught of the collective will of the Transmitters. I knew I didn't have much time to do what I needed to do.

Ketch sensed what I was going to do. He let go of Ivey and rushed toward me but I had already begun to run across the room and gained just enough momentum by the time I reached the window. I heard Ketch and Ivey scream in unison as I plunged through the glass.

I tried to look back but found I could only see out of one eye. Glass was embedded in the other. I think time moved slower as I sailed into the air. I poised for a moment in the sunlight and looked at the open sky … feeling peaceful … then time caught up with me and my stomach did a funny somersault as I plunged seven stories to the dirty pavement.

****

Ketch ended his cell phone call with a satisfied grunt. He and Ivey had gathered and trained a powerful force of psychics and soldiers. He and his highest ranking officers had overseen loading the weapons in the simple, industrial-looking grey vans just hours ago.

Thanks to Lucas, the world now knew the truth about Urbania and of the threat the Great City posed. However, so much was still a mystery. A full-on assault would be met with unknown Urbanian weapons. Lucas, Ivey and Ketch simply did not know what kind of physical destruction Urbania was capable of imposing. So, with the help of the UN, Ketch and Ivey led a resistance … an unexpectedly small but powerful resistance to be followed by a larger one once Urbania showed what she had up her sleeve. It was a dangerous mission but it could not be led by anyone more determined than Ketch.

"Is everyone ready to move out, Commander Gault?" Ketch asked the craggy, seasoned soldier he'd chosen to be in command.

"Yes, Sir, on your order, Sir," Gault snapped off a salute. Ketch acknowledged it off-handedly. He was not military and didn't really feel comfortable being saluted but it was Gault's way so he accepted it.

He went in search of Ivey and found her coming out of the bunker they had shared on the base for the past several months. Her dark hair had been cut and styled with bangs to hide the scar on her forehead. She looked fresh and as beautiful to him as the first time he ever saw her. His tender thoughts dissipated when he saw she had been crying.

"There's no telling how many times this letter has been forwarded. It's a miracle it reached us at all," Ivey said, sniffing. She held out a sheet of paper.

Ketch read the letter and fought back the threat of tears thick in his throat.

"I can't believe it. Lucas has been nominated for a Pulitzer for the story on Urbania. Oh, how I wish he could be here now to see this," Ivey whispered.

A muscle tensed in Ketch's jaw as he continued to fight his emotions. Ivey placed a hand on his arm. Ketch's voice was raw with unexpressed emotion when he finally spoke. "He knows. Somehow, he knows all about this and he's smiling."

Later, as the determined caravan pulled out of the secret military base, Ketch was stunned by a brilliant sunrise lighting the Nevada desert. Next to him, Ivey sighed and he knew she felt the power and the beauty as strongly as he did …

… and he vaguely wondered at how a sunrise could look so beautiful just before the onset of a war.

The End

ABOUT THE AUTHOR

L.A. Story is a professional daydreamer and a naturalized Mississippian. She lives in an enchanted forest with her husband, a shaman poet, and two small dogs who believe they are vicious wolves. She lives near her four brilliant children, of whom she believes are scary smart with world domination potential. Among said children, two have managed to produce two grandchildren who are possessed of an equally frightening intellect.

L.A. has been creating stories in her head and attempting to put them on paper since she was old enough hold a pencil. She has been an award-winning staff writer and columnist for a local newspaper. Her poetry and fiction has also been published in numerous publications. She teaches poetry workshops for the Crossroads Poetry Project and works as editor of a paranormal romance magazine called "Trysts of Fate" (Alban Lake Publishing). She is currently working on her first full length novel, The Gifted, which is to be released in June 2015 (River Oaks Press).

ACKNOWLEDGEMENTS

L.A. Story would like to acknowledge that the original edition of *Urbania* was published February, 2006 by Sam's Dot Publishing. This is a revised, second edition.

Cover photographic art and design by L.A. Story and Keith W. Sikora.

COMING SOON

JUNE 2015:

The Gifted: Adversaries & Healers

By L.A. Story

Rachel Hannah is funny and kind. She is a second grade teacher who lives an ordinary life until she meets Sage Waldron. She is swept away by this mysterious man. What she doesn't know is that he is an Adversary and she is his "mission." Rachel is caught between two immeasurably powerful forces and will soon make a series of choices that will affect her future and Sage's and will begin to tip the scales between good and evil.

There is a war going between the Adversaries and the Healers and the general population is mercifully unaware.

There are those walking among us whose destiny will affect the fate of us all. Those people are not aware of their potential until they accept the power and the burden of The Gift.

JANUARY 2016

Book II of *The Gifted* Trilogy

CRIERS: Rise of the Prophets

By L.A. Story

Duke Batten, the infamous California street preacher, is the first of the Criers -- powerful prophets in the quickly escalating war between the Adversaries and the Healers who fight for the forces of Light and Dark. More and more Criers are appearing and some are the most unlikely individuals one would expect to be called into service by the King of Light.

Sage and Rachel Waldron are a powerful force for the Healers, along with their children, 26 year old Daniel, and 24 year old Sarah. The Adversaries have become more desperate as the Healers have begun to win too many skirmishes. In a bold move, the Adversaries employ a terrible strategy to turn the tide of the war. As part of this strategy, Duke Batten and his family, as well as the Waldron family become primary targets.

JUNE 2016

The third and final book of the epic *Gifted* Trilogy

BEYOND SHAMMUA

By L.A. Story

The year is 2303 and battle-hardened Caleb O'Shea, a descendant of Sage Waldron, has been working as a mercenary as he consistently denies the heritage of his family's powerful bloodline. However, a high-ranking politician has hired him to follow a member of an undeclared warrior species. They have nicknamed the being "Attila,' and it is Caleb's job to find out where this being, and the others like him, go when they leave Earth.

Caleb accepts the mission and discovers a terrifying truth that forces him to embrace his enormous power and reconcile him with the part he is destined to play in the war for the salvation or damnation of humankind.

If you liked the novella Urbania, *then don't miss out on the novel:*

DECEMBER 2016:

BREAKERS

A novel by L.A. Story

Ivey is a counselor at Urbania's Education Center when an angry young man named Noah Ketchum is brought to her to be re-educated or be sentenced to a Breaker's punishment. As she gets to know "Ketch," she begins to realize he has abilities above anything anyone has ever seen. As she earns his trust, he confides what he believes is happening in Urbania.

At first, Ivey believes Ketch is paranoid and dangerous … until she begins to find evidence that he may be right and the Urbanian leadership wants him for their own terrifying agenda. Those who rise up against the Great City are called "Breakers" and the punishment is dire. Ivey and Ketch will risk their lives in a fight for the rights of everyone to have a choice as to whether or not they want to become part of Urbania's doctrine.

COPYRIGHT NOTICE

© 2015 by L.A. Story
River Oaks Press
All Rights Reserved

www.ingramcontent.com/pod-product-compliance
Lightning Source LLC
Chambersburg PA
CBHW060955120626
46557CB00003B/1163